MISOSO

ONCE UPON A TIME
TALES FROM AFRICA

RETOLD BY VERNA AARDEMA
ILLUSTRATED BY REYNOLD RUFFINS

SCHOLASTIC INC.

NEW YORK   TORONTO   LONDON   AUCKLAND   SYDNEY

To Loree Chase and her fourth graders—V. A.

To Ranger and Rebecca—R. R.

The illustrations for this book were done in pencil and acrylic paints.

ISBN 0-590-67307-6

Text copyright © 1994 by Verna Aardema.
Illustrations copyright © 1994 by Reynolds Ruffins.
All rights reserved. Published by Scholastic Inc., 555 Broadway, New York,
NY 10012, by arrangement with Alfred A. Knopf, Inc.

12 11 10 9 8 7 6 5 4 3 2 1   6 7 8 9/9 0 1/0

Printed in the U.S.A.   08

First Scholastic printing, February 1996

CONTENTS

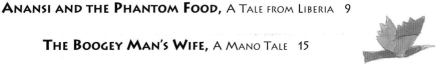

FOREWORD

Misoso (me-SAW-saw) are the "Once upon a time" tales of Africa. The word misoso, which comes from the Mbundu ('m-BOON-doo) tribe of Angola, describes stories told mostly for entertainment. The stories in this collection were selected with that in mind; if they teach a lesson, or illuminate the culture of a people, that is a plus.

In Angola, they use formulas for their misoso tales. The storyteller begins, "Let me tell you a story about . . ." and ends with "I have told my story. It is finished."

INTRODUCTION

"The nose does not know the flavor of the salt," the Hausa people say. Likewise, few of us can know the flavor of a tale told in the native tongue under an African moon. The African storyteller performs a story as if it were a play, taking all the parts himself. He imitates the cries of animals and gives each character a different voice. Also, he involves his listeners—eliciting clapping and noises, and letting them chime in on repeated refrains.

To get close to an African flavor, I have retold tales from *early* sources that were recorded in a native language and then translated into English. Three of the following stories are from the earliest such books. "Toad's Trick" is from a book published in 1854, only the second book of this kind; "The Cock and the Jackal" is from 1864, the fourth; and "No, Boconono!" is from 1868, the fifth.

Because these stories are from early sources, it happens that they are all from the perimeter of that part of Africa which is south of the Sahara Desert. The first European trading posts and settlements were along the coast. Later, missionaries and anthropologists followed the traders and settlers. And it is from their writings that material for this book was obtained.

The tales are arranged geographically. So one can take a literary jaunt beginning with the Temnes of Sierra Leone, down the west coast to the Khoikhoi of Southwest Africa; then up the east coast, beginning with the Zulus of South Africa, north to the Swahilis of the eastern African coast; then westward overland to the Emo-Yo-Quaim of Nigeria.

My love of folk stories began in childhood with *Andersen's Fairytales,* the first book I remember owning. I recall sitting in my little red rocker, night after night, with "The Little Mermaid." My sister, Sally, and two little brothers would be drifting off to sleep in our big room. After finishing the story, in tears because of the sad ending, I would crawl into bed with Sally.

The retelling of African folktales just evolved for me. I've wanted to be a writer since I was eleven years old, and at Michigan State College I took every writing course in the catalogue.

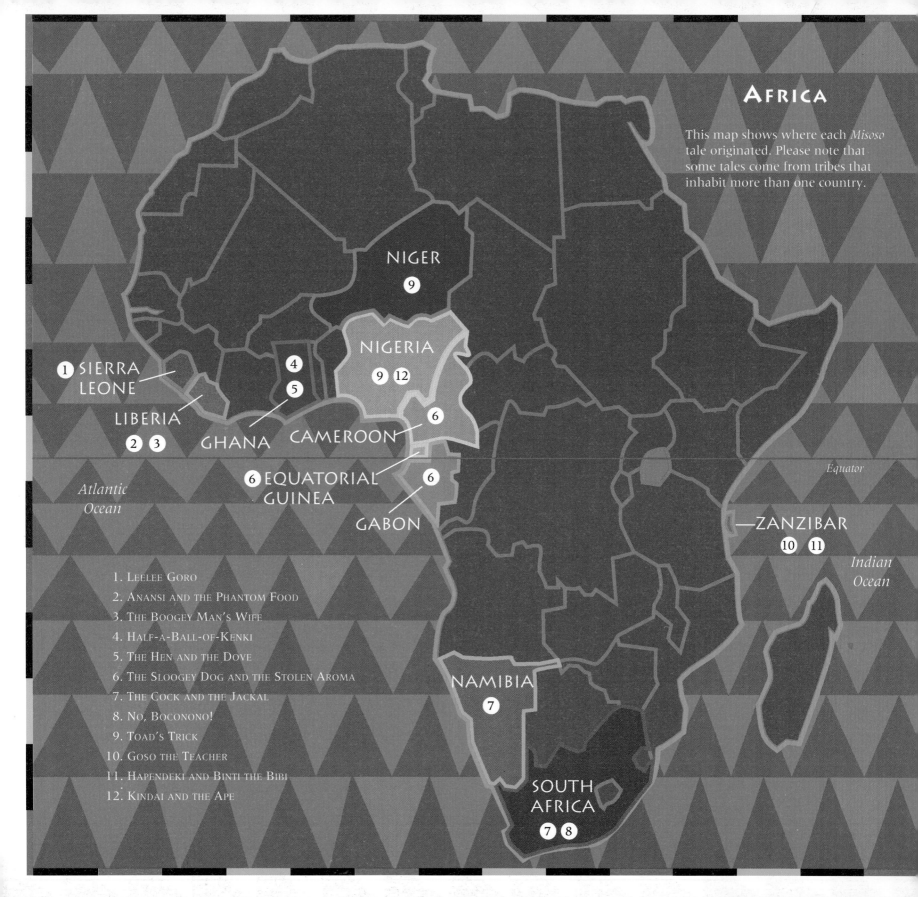

AFRICA

This map shows where each *Misoso* tale originated. Please note that some tales come from tribes that inhabit more than one country.

NIGER
9

NIGERIA
9 12

(1) SIERRA LEONE

4

LIBERIA

5

2 3

GHANA

CAMEROON

6

(6) EQUATORIAL GUINEA

6

GABON

Atlantic Ocean

Equator

ZANZIBAR

10 11

Indian Ocean

1. LEELEE GORO
2. ANANSI AND THE PHANTOM FOOD
3. THE BOOGEY MAN'S WIFE
4. HALF-A-BALL-OF-KENKI
5. THE HEN AND THE DOVE
6. THE SLOOGEY DOG AND THE STOLEN AROMA
7. THE COCK AND THE JACKAL
8. NO, BOCONONO!
9. TOAD'S TRICK
10. GOSO THE TEACHER
11. HAPENDEKI AND BINTI THE BIBI
12. KINDAI AND THE APE

NAMIBIA

7

SOUTH AFRICA

7 8

But my interest in Africa came after college, when I systematically began to "read around the world," and became fascinated with that intricately diverse continent.

I did not think about writing for children until after my second child was born. Paula would not eat without a story. At first I would tell her familiar tales like "Little Red Riding Hood." But soon, I began to make up my own. Because I was always reading books about Africa, the "feeding" stories were usually set in that land.

I thought one of those stories was good enough to try to sell. I did sell it, too, to *The Instructor* magazine. More important than that, the editor at Coward–McCann suggested that I use it as chapter one of a juvenile novel. Right off, I could not think of chapter two. So I offered, instead, to do a collection of African folktales. Ultimately, the result was my first book, *Tales from the Story Hat*. And I have stayed in the never-never land of the folk story ever since.

I have put together this collection of tales to give readers familiar with my picture books something of mine to grow into—something to nourish their growing interest in Africa. It is in answer to those boys and girls who have been asking me, "Do you ever write BIG books?"

In Africa, stories are usually told at night around a fire, or within a circle of fires. Often anyone in the audience—man, woman, or child—who has a tale to tell will volunteer or be asked to tell it. Those especially gifted in the art become village storytellers. Some of them become professionals who earn their living by entertaining from village to village.

More than a hundred years ago, Hidorro Kabbo, a San storyteller, said, "When one is traveling along a road, he can sit down and wait for a story to overtake him."

Here one has only to turn a page.

GLOSSARY

Leelee: Temne for *little*

Goro: Temne for *girl*

Temne (TEM-nay): An African tribe who live south
of the Sierra Leone River in Sierra Leone

Mmapp (mmahp): An ideophone, an onomatopoetic
word, for *falling*

LEELEE GORO

A TEMNE TALE

IN THE BEGINNING, WHEN THE EARTH WAS SET DOWN AND THE SKY was lifted up, some things were not quite finished. It was during that time that the animals gathered together for a meeting.

The first night a big rain put out all their fires.

The next morning they shivered, *tir-r-r-r!* They had no fire to warm themselves. Presently they saw smoke rising from a little hut on a nearby hillside. Lion said, "Antelope, go fetch fire for us."

The antelope went. He said to the woman at

the house, "Morning, Mammy. I've come to ask for fire."

"I don't begrudge anyone fire," said the woman. "But I have one law here. The person who gets fire from me must fight my child and beat her."

The antelope asked, "Where is your child who fights?"

Mammy pointed to a small, small girl who was playing with her doll by the fire. She said, "See that leelee girl? That's the one."

Antelope said, "Mammy, you want me to fight that little girl? You want me to kill your daughter?"

Mammy said, "Never mind about that. The sand behind the house is the fighting place. Come along."

They went behind the house. And Mammy sang this magic song:

"Goro, Leelee Goro,
Fight 'im, Leelee Goro;
Heave 'im high, to the sky,
So he won't come back till tomorrow."

Then Leelee Goro took hold of the antelope's leg and swung him—WEO—so high, he was almost gone! When he came down, he got his mouth full of sand. That made him cough, *kaa, kaa, kaa.* And to this day, antelopes cough.

Antelope went back without the fire.

The animals were disappointed. But then Leopard announced that he would try. He went to the woman and said, "Mammy, I've come for fire."

The woman said, "All right. But you'll have to fight my child."

They went out to the fighting place. And Mammy sang:

"Goro, Leelee Goro,
Fight 'im, Leelee Goro;
Heave 'im high, to the sky,
So he won't come back till tomorrow."

Leelee Goro grabbed that leopard and pitched him higher than the hill. He fell on a hard place, and the blood spattered all over him. And to this day, the leopard has a spotted coat.

When the other animals saw the leopard coming with his coat spattered with blood, they said, "We'll get no fire today."

Then Elephant came forward swinging his trunk. He said, "I'll get that fire! I'll wrap my trunk around that little girl. I'll throw her up! I'll whop her down! I'll get that fire!" Then he rooted up a tree to show how strong he was.

Elephant went to the woman and said, "Mammy, I've come to fight that little girl for the fire."

Mammy said, "All right. Come to the fighting place." Then she sang:

"Goro, Leelee Goro,
Fight 'im, Leelee Goro;
Heave 'im high, to the sky,
So he won't come back till tomorrow."

Elephant was very heavy. But by the power of the magic song, Leelee Goro threw him up higher than a palm tree. When he fell, he hurt his two front teeth. The teeth swelled bigger and bigger, and longer and longer. And because of that, all elephants have two long tusks.

Elephant went back without the fire.

Then Spider said he would try. The animals laughed, *nge, nge, nge*. And Lion said, "Do you see what happened to those big animals? Do you really think you can do what they could not? Well, go try."

Spider told the woman, "Mammy, I've come for fire."

Mammy said, "All right. Go fight my child." And she sang:

"Goro, Leelee Goro,
Fight 'im, Leelee Goro;
Heave 'im high, to the sky,
So he won't come back till tomorrow."

Leelee Goro put that spider on her thumb and flipped him up. When he fell, his feet split, TIK! No more did he have two hands and two feet—he had eight feet! But they were not strong. And that is why spiders have to crawl now.

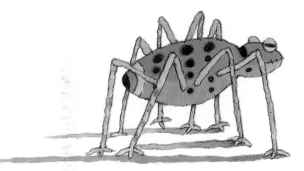

Spider crawled back without the fire.

Then Conk the snail said he would try. The animals laughed, *gug, gug, gug*, and Lion said, "How can you be so foolish! Don't you see what happened to Spider?" He whacked the snail on his back, marring Conk's shell. And to this day snails carry the mark of that blow on their backs.

But that did not deter the snail, for he had a plan. First he went to the fighting place and walked up and down, rubbing slippery spit all over it. Then he went to the door and said, "Mammy, I've come for fire."

Mammy said, "All right. Go fight." She did not even bother to sing.

Conk hurried to the fighting place. He stood in the middle of the slippery spot. When Leelee Goro came, she put one foot into the spit, and MMAPP! She went sprawling!

5

Then Conk took hold of her and threw her up so high her mother could not see her! Mammy began to cry. And that brought crying into the world.

Conk took the fire back. At last the beasts cooked and ate—all before Leelee Goro even came down!

When Leelee Goro finally fell, she cried too, *wolu, wolu, wolu.*

Then Mammy hugged Leelee Goro. And Leelee Goro hugged Mammy. And they both stopped crying. So, although they brought crying into the world, they also brought a way to stop it. For it is still true that people stop crying when they are hugged.

AFTERWORD

"Leelee Goro" is a *pourquoi* tale—that is, a tale that explains why things are as they are. It is unusual in that it relates the origins of not one but eight different phenomena. While the theme of how the leopard got his spots is common all over Africa—some tribes have several different versions of that—the story of what brought crying into the world and what can stop it is unique to this particular tale.

The close relationship between mother and daughter that lies at the heart of "Leelee Goro" is characteristic of the Temne tribe's folklore and way of life. The female Temne child works beside her mother as soon as she is big enough to stir the stew or to carry her baby brother.

GLOSSARY

Anansi (A-NAHN-see): One of the names of the spider of West African folklore

Liberia (Li-BEER-ee-uh): A small country on the west coast of Africa that was founded by freed American slaves

Hungry time: The dry season

Cassava (cuh-SAH-vuh): A plant with a fleshy edible root that is cooked as a vegetable, or dried and made into flour or tapioca

Plantain (PLAN-tin): A large, coarse type of banana that needs to be cooked to be palatable

ANANSI AND THE PHANTOM FOOD

A TALE FROM LIBERIA

IT WAS A VERY BAD "HUNGRY TIME." ANANSI'S PEOPLE WERE ON THE VERGE of starvation. So one day he called them together and said, "I am going to a far place to find food for us because nothing I can do here will help."

"Good, good," said the people. "If you find anything at all, hurry back and tell us."

Anansi's wife, Aso, gave him a few kernels of corn to sustain him on the way, and he set out. He walked many miles, till at last he saw smoke rising from a distant village. He put his eyes on the smoke and hurried toward it. To his surprise, it was a town where cassava lived—just cassava!

One cassava said, "Well, Spider, welcome! We are waiting to be eaten. You want to eat us roasted, fried, or boiled?"

Anansi said, "No matter. Myself, I am so hungry I could eat you any way at all."

Then the cassava roasted themselves so that Anansi could eat them.

The spider was just sitting down to his meal, when he saw a column of smoke on the horizon. He asked, "My people, who lives at that far place?"

A cassava said, "That's the town where the plantains live."

"OOOOOH!" cried Anansi. He started to get

up because he liked plantains better than cassava. In fact, he ate cassava only when there was nothing else to be had.

"Spider, don't go!" cried the cassava. "Please eat us first."

But Anansi was already on his way. He did not even look back when a cassava said, "Oh, no! Now we have to wait all over again." He just put his eyes on that smoke and hurried toward it.

When he reached that village, the plantains came rushing to him from all sides. They said, "Well, Spider, welcome! We are waiting to be eaten. You want to eat us roasted, fried, or boiled?"

Anansi said, "No matter. Myself, I am so hungry I could eat you any way at all."

Then the plantains fried themselves so that he could eat them.

Anansi was just sitting down to eat the plantains, when he saw smoke on the horizon. He asked, "My people, who lives at that far place?"

The plantains said, "That's the town where the rice live."

"OOOOOH!" cried Anansi. He started to get up because he liked rice even better than plantains.

The cooked plantains said, "Spider, don't go yet! You must eat us first. See how brown we are! See how juicy we are!"

But the spider had already hurried off, thinking about the rice in that village farther on. He put his eyes on the column of smoke and hurried toward it. At last he reached the place.

The rice people said, "Well, Spider, welcome! We are waiting to be eaten. You want to eat us roasted, fried, or boiled?"

"No matter," said Anansi. "Myself, I am so hungry I could eat you any way at all."

Then the rice boiled themselves so that he could eat them.

Anansi was just sitting down before a big bowl of rice with the steam coming up, when he saw a column of smoke on the horizon. He asked, "My people, who lives at that far place?"

The rice said, "We don't know who lives there."

"Hmmm," said Anansi. "Maybe that's the town where the meat lives. You know, the juicy red meat. I can almost smell it cooking."

But the rice said, "We don't know who lives there. That place is too far. We never go there."

The thought of meat waiting to be eaten filled Anansi's mind. He got up and left without eating any rice at all. He was so hungry for meat he just put his eyes on that small cloud of smoke and hurried toward it. All the time, he was picturing in his mind a chunk of meat cooking on a stick with the juices dripping into the fire, *sst, sst, sst.*

Anansi walked and walked. And at last he reached the place. At the village gate, he stopped. He rubbed his eyes. He could not believe what he was seeing! It was his *own* village! This was more than he could stand. There, just inside the gate, he fell *mmapp* in a faint.

When he woke up, Aso gave him a bowl of fish bone soup. He felt a little better then. But after he told her about the towns where there was food waiting to be eaten, she walked off saying, "Who travels alone tells many a lie."

The villagers did not believe Anansi either. And he could not prove his story, because never again was he able to find those villages where the cassava, the plantains, and the rice lived—all of them just waiting to be eaten.

AFTERWORD

Spider stories can be found along the west coast of Africa, from Sierra Leone to Ghana. The spider—called Anansi, Nansii, or sometimes Father Spider—may be either a spider or a man, as he is in this tale.

In a typical Anansi story, the spider is greedy, lazy, and mischievous, using his wits to escape punishment for his tricks. For example, in one tale he begs an angry mob to throw him into a fire rather than a river. He pleads, "In the fire, I would ascend to the sky in smoke . . . But drowning in the river is not good." Predictably, the people toss him into the river. But Anansi has the last laugh as he runs off on the river's surface, calling, "You foolish people, don't you know that water is the spider's friend?"

This particular spider story presents a different Anansi, one who sets out to help his community yet fails miserably. It is as if Anansi cannot be good, no matter how hard he tries.

GLOSSARY

Mano (MAHN-oh): An indigenous tribe of Liberia

Goma (GO-mah): Liberian pidgin English for *go away*

Da: An affectionate term for *Father*

THE BOOGEY MAN'S WIFE

A MANO TALE

IN THE OLD DAYS, IN MANO HOUSE-
HOLDS IN LIBERIA, CHILDREN WERE
taught strict obedience to their parents. And
when daughters married, they were expected to
obey their husbands.

But when the young and beautiful Goma was
given to the old and ugly Boogey Man—in
exchange for a night's lodging!—there was
trouble ahead.

In those days, the only roads in the jungle
were the paths made by elephants. People
walked to market on the elephant paths, and

they always tried to get home before dark.

But one day a man named Da stayed too long at the market. On his way home, night overtook him. It was so dark on the path he could not see his own self. He had to feel his way.

Suddenly, out of the dark came the HUNN . . . HUNN of a prowling lion. Da was terrified. But soon, in the distance, he spied the light of a cooking fire shining through the doorway of a hut. Da called, "Help!"

A man put his head out of the door. "What's the matter out there?" he asked.

"A lion is stalking me!" cried Da. "Will you let me come in?"

"Come in, stranger," said the man.

Da ducked through the low doorway. A kettle steamed on the cooking stones, and Da could smell rice and meat and peppers stewing. He thought for a minute; then he said, "Wo! It's scary out there! If you will let me stay here tonight, I will give you my beautiful daughter, Goma, for a wife."

"Look at me," said the man. "Are you sure you want me for a son-in-law? I'm so ugly people call me Boogey Man."

Da looked at the man. He *was* ugly. His face was as wrinkled as a cassava root. His beady

eyes were sunken under bushy brows. And his ears stuck out like the ears of an angry elephant.

But when Da thought about the danger on the path, the man did not look so bad. Da said, "A handsome face means nothing. If you will let me stay, I'll know that you are kind. I want my daughter to have a kind husband." He put out his hand to seal the bargain.

"Hold it, man," said Boogey Man. "Is this daughter of yours obedient? I would not want a disobedient wife."

"Obedient!" cried Da. "She's the most obedient girl in all Africa! She does everything I ask her to do."

"Then I agree," said Boogey Man.

So the two shook hands, and Da shared the stew, and when it was time to sleep, he lay down on one of the low clay beds along the walls of the hut.

When the pepper bird sang and dawn lighted the doorway, Boogey Man said, "Let's go get that wife you promised to give me."

The two set out down the elephant path toward Da's house. When they arrived, Da called, "Goma, come out and see the husband I brought you."

Goma came out. Da said, "Goma, this is

17

Boogey Man, your husband."

When Boogey Man's eyes sat down on Goma, his smile was like the sun coming up. He cried, "Goma, you're pretty as a sunbird! Shake hands with me!"

But Goma put her hands behind her and said, "No!"

Boogey Man shook his finger in Da's face. He said:

"I saved your life,
And you promised to
Give me Goma for a wife.
Now, she won't even
Shake hands with me!"

Da said, "Goma, shake hands with him."
Goma did.

The two men talked a little longer. And when Boogey Man was ready to go, he called, "Come, Goma, my wife. Come home with me."

But Goma said, "No!"

Boogey Man said to Da:

"I saved your life,
And you promised to
Give me Goma for a wife.

Now, she won't even
Come home with me!"

Da's eyes died for shame. He said, "Goma, go home with him!"

Then Goma followed Boogey Man down the elephant path to his house. When they arrived, Boogey Man said, "The hut is dirty. It never had a woman to clean it before." He held out a broom and said, "Goma, be a good wife and sweep the floor."

But Goma said, "No!"

Boogey Man went back to Da. He said:

"I saved your life,
And you promised to
Give me Goma for a wife.
Now, she won't even
Sweep my floor."

Da went to Boogey Man's house. He said, "Goma, sweep that floor!"

Goma began to sweep. *Pas, pas, pas*, went the palm leaf broom.

When Goma had finished, Boogey Man found his short-handled hoe. He said, "At last I have a woman to scratch-farm for me. Here,

Goma, be a good wife and hoe the yam patch."

But Goma said, "No!"

Boogey Man went back to Da. He said:

"I saved your life,
And you promised to
Give me Goma for a wife.
Now, she won't even
Hoe my yam patch!"

Da went to Boogey Man's house. He said, "Goma, hoe that yam patch!"

Goma began to hoe. *Kok, kok, kok*, went the little hoe. Now and then, with her fingers, she plucked out a weed that was too close to a yam plant.

Boogey Man was pleased. He said, "I see that you know how to hoe, Goma. You'll make a good wife yet."

"Tuh!" said Goma.

But she was working. So Boogey Man left her and went to look at his rabbit traps. Soon he returned with a rabbit. "Look, Goma," he cried, "see the fine fat rabbit I caught. Cook it for me."

But Goma said, "No!"

Boogey Man gave a big sigh, *uuhuuu!* Then he went back to Da and said:

"I saved your life,
And you promised to
Give me Goma for a wife.
Now, she won't even
Cook my rabbit!"

Da went to Boogey Man's house. He said, "Goma, cook that rabbit!"

Goma made a fire. And at long last, she had the rabbit boiling, *pon, pon, pon,* in the big black pot. When the meat was cooked, she called, "Boogey Man, your chop is ready."

While Boogey Man ate, Goma walked back and forth before the hut. She cried softly to herself, *du, du, du.* She said, "I don't like to be the wife of Boogey Man. He orders me about all day. I wish I could go home to my father."

When Boogey Man had finished eating, he called, "Goma, come and see. I left as much meat for you as I ate myself. Eat it and grow fat!"

But Goma said, "No!"

Boogey Man set out for Da's house. But this time he went a roundabout way. He went first to the home of a wise old woman named Mammy Mamina.

Mammy Mamina was pounding mealies in her yard, *puh, puh, puh.* She saw him coming, and she said, "It isn't one thing. It isn't two things. It's Boogey Man himself!"

"Grandmother," said Boogey Man, "trouble has caught me. I have a wife who won't do anything I ask her to do. What should I do about it?"

"Complain to her father," said Mammy Mamina. Then she went back to pounding her mealies, *puh, puh, puh.*

Boogey Man went on to Da's house. Da saw him coming. He called, "What won't Goma do now?"

Boogey Man said:

"I saved your life,
And you promised to
Give me Goma for a wife.
Now, she won't even
Eat!"

Da went to Boogey Man's house. He cried, "Goma, *eat!*"

Goma began to eat. And while she was

eating, Boogey Man walked back and forth before the hut. He said to himself, "That Goma. She's the worst wife in all Africa. Obedient? She's more trouble than a treeful of monkeys! I'm going to tell her something."

Boogey Man stormed into the hut. He cried, "Goma, I've had enough of your stubbornness. Go home to your father."

"I'll go," cried Goma. She jumped up and ran, *kata, kata, kata,* down the elephant path.

"She obeyed me!" cried Boogey Man. "I didn't even have to go and get Da. Wo! That was foolish of me. I let her go just when she started to obey me!"

AFTERWORD

This tale comes from Liberia, a country founded by freed American slaves who returned to Africa. Those slaves spoke English, and the term *Boogey Man* was in their vocabulary. Both white Americans and their slaves frightened children into behaving with the threat "The Boogey Man will get you if you don't watch out!" The Mano storyteller probably learned the expression from his American-Liberian neighbors.

Characters similar to the Boogey Man could be found in other tribes. The Ashanti kept children in their huts at night by telling them that if they went out, Sasabonsum would grab them up in his long arms and fly off with them. Nandi parents warned that the devil Chemosit was always lurking about, seeking to devour bad children. And the San hushed their children's cries by telling them, "Whitemouth will hear you, and he'll come and swallow you whole!"

When she was young, a child like Goma would have heard Boogey Man threats many times. For her father to bargain her off to a man with that name was going too far—which is probably what gave her the courage to defy him. Among the Mano, a woman was supposed to do as her husband said, even if she knew a better way.

GLOSSARY

Kenki (KEN-kee): Cold cornmeal mush

Ashanti (A-SHAHN-tee): An African tribe living in Ghana

Yo: An exclamation

Kye, kye, kye (k-YEH, k-YEH, k-YEH): Ha, ha, ha

Gben (g-BEN): Ding-dong

Sah: Ashanti for *sic 'em*

Kuputu (koo-POO-too): Ideophone for *galloping*

Pamdal (PAHM-dahl): Ideophone for *headlong*

Kpong (k-PONG): Ideophone for *a round-and-round movement*

Dadwa (DAD-wah): Ideophone for *falling*

Nkatee (n-KAH-tay): Ashanti for *peanut*

Kwadu (QUAH-doo): Ashanti for *banana*

Fu-fu (FOO-foo): Mashed yams or mashed bananas

Kpung (k-PUNG): Ideophone for *unwinding*

HALF-A-BALL-OF-KENKI

AN ASHANTI TALE

I DO NOT MEAN, I DO NOT REALLY MEAN THAT THIS STORY IS TRUE.

Long ago and far away, Fly and Leopard were friends. One day Leopard said, "Fly, let's go looking for brides."

"Yo!" cried Fly. "That will be fun for me. The girls are sure to like me better than you."

Leopard laughed, *kye, kye, kye.* He said, "We shall see!" Then he bathed and oiled his fur. He even put a gold chain around his neck, and anklets with bells of gold on his front feet. To make sure his friend did not outshine him, he

tied up his dirty old sleeping mat and gave it to Fly to carry on his head.

The two set out down the path, Leopard's gold bells singing, *gben, gben, gben,* as they walked along.

Presently they came to a village. Fly entered first. He put down his burden and said to the people in the plaza, "Mothers all and fathers all, I give you morning greetings."

The people greeted him in return, and the young girls gathered about him.

Then Leopard entered through the gate, jingling his anklets with every step, *gben, gben.* He smiled a crafty smile and said, "Mothers all and fathers all—"

But the chief cried, "Off with you! How dare you enter our village!" Then he shouted, "SAH!" to his dog, and the dog bolted after the leopard. Leopard went flying out of the gate, *kuputu, kuputu.*

Fly followed him, and the two went on. At length they came to another town. Again Fly entered first. The people greeted him, and the young girls clustered around him. But when Leopard arrived, he was driven away just as before.

Back on the path, Leopard said, "Look here, Fly! Give me that old mat, and you take these gold things and adorn yourself. We shall see if it is because of the mat that the girls like you."

So, with Fly wearing the gold ornaments and Leopard carrying the mat, they went on their way. When they reached the next village, Leopard entered first with the dirty old mat on his head. He said, "Mothers all and fathers all, I give you midday greetings."

But the women and children screamed and ran, *pamdal,* into their houses. Then, when the men grabbed their spears, Leopard scuttled away so fast that the mat fell off his head.

A small time later, Leopard watched through a crack in the fence as Fly entered the plaza and was welcomed by the people.

Leopard heard a maiden say, "Tih, tih! How handsome you look with those gold things on. If it were not for the beating I would get, I would run away with you."

Leopard turned his back on them in disgust. He sang:

"When the moon is out,
The stars are dim.
And I can't go looking for girls
With a handsome man like him!"

When Fly joined Leopard on the path, Leopard was overcome by jealousy. He cried, "Stand still, Fly. Take off those gold things and give them to me quickly, quickly, quickly."

As the fly was slipping them off, the leopard plucked a long creeper. Then he grabbed the fly and bound him to a palm tree—winding the vine

around him and the tree, *kpong, kpong, kpong.* And he hid himself nearby.

Presently Nkatee the peanut came down the path on her way to market. She was stepping daintily, *pip, pip, pip,* over the roots that criss-crossed the path. She saw the bundle on the tree and asked, "Who is hanging there so very black? Who is hanging there so very glossy?"

Fly sang:

"It's I, the fly, tied
By Leopard to this tree,
Because the girls hated him,
But they loved me.
Please come here and set me free!"

But Nkatee said, "If I set you free, Leopard will make peanut soup of me." And she hurried off, *pip-pip-pip-pip, pip, pip, pip.*

Soon Kwadu the banana came striding by, *tuk-pik, tuk-pik.* She saw the bundle on the tree and asked, "Who is hanging there so very black? Who is hanging there so very glossy?"

Fly sang:

"It's I, the fly, tied
By Leopard to this tree,

Because the girls hated him,
But they loved me.
Please come here and set me free!"

But Kwadu said, "If I loosened you, Leopard would mash me to fu-fu!" And she hurried off, *tuk-pik, tuk-pik, tuk-pik.*

At last there came along Dokonfa, half a ball of kenki. Half-a-Ball-of-Kenki was singing:

"I'm Half-a-Ball-of-Kenki,
Which is better than none.
I'm Half-a-Ball-of-Kenki,
And two of me makes one."

Then she saw the bundle on the tree and asked, "Who is hanging there so very black? Who is hanging there so very glossy?"

"It's I, the fly, tied
By Leopard to this tree,
Because the girls hated him,
But they loved me.
Please come here and set me free!"

Half-a-Ball-of-Kenki said, "I have heard you. And I shall set you free." She reached up and unwound the creeper, *kpung, kpung, kpung.*

And the fly flew off with a *zzzzz!*

Then Leopard leaped out of the bushes. He bellowed, "Why have you freed my man?"

"Well, I have done it," said Half-a-Ball-of-Kenki. "And what you will do to me, do."

"You and I will fight," said Leopard.

Half-a-Ball-of-Kenki said, "It is already early evening. If we are going to fight, let us make a fire first."

So they broke wood and set it alight in the middle of the path. Then they began to wrestle. Round and round they tumbled. Soon Leopard tore Half-a-Ball-of-Kenki from him and threw her *blim*, against a tree.

"A thing like that is nothing," said Half-a-Ball-of-Kenki as she pulled herself together.

They fought again. And Leopard slammed Half-a-Ball-of-Kenki deep into the sand. *Ras, ras, ras,* she dug herself out, and brushed herself off. Then she said, "Now, we'll really fight! That was just for practice."

They grappled again, rolling on the ground— *dadwa, dadwa, dadwa!* Then, suddenly, Half-a-Ball-of-Kenki gathered all her strength, lifted up the leopard, and threw him into the fire!

"I'm out! I'm out! I'm out!" cried the leopard. And that is how the leopard got his cry. When he came out of the fire, there were black spots where the charred wood had touched him. There were white spots where the ashes had touched him. And that is how the leopard got a spotted coat.

To this day, flies sit upon the leaves in which kenki has been wrapped. They are saying thank you because of what Half-a-Ball-of-Kenki did for Fly long ago.

This is my story. If it be sweet, or if it be not sweet, take some and let the rest come back to me.

AFTERWORD

This is a tongue-in-cheek tale from the far side of the imagination. It demonstrates what can happen when the limitations of style and substance are ignored.

The opening formula shows that listeners were not meant to take the story literally. The African storyteller probably performed it like a play, imitating the movements of the leopard, the dainty walk of the peanut, and the contortions of Half-a-Ball-of-Kenki as she pulls herself together. And Fly's cumulative refrain and Half-a-Ball-of-Kenki's song gave the listeners ample opportunity to participate.

GLOSSARY

Akoko (a-KOH-koh): Ashanti for *hen*

Aturukuku (a-TOO-roo-KOO-koo): Ashanti for *dove*

Bush rope: Any wild vine flexible enough to use as rope

THE HEN AND THE DOVE

AN ASHANTI FABLE

ONE DAY AKOKO THE HEN SAID TO ATURUKUKU THE DOVE, "YOU GO TO the tall grass country and I will go to the village of men. If you find plenty of food, come and tell me. And if I find plenty of food, I will come and tell you."

Aturukuku flew off. And Akoko went to the village of men. Soon she was caught by a woman and tied to a tree near the woman's hut.

The hen did not like having the bush rope on her leg. But she got used to it. And she did like having a water dish nearby, and the grain and food scraps that the woman brought her.

One day Aturukuku came to visit her. She perched on a limb of the tree to which Akoko was tied. Akoko asked, "My friend, did you find food plentiful in the tall grass country?"

A-kuu, a-kuu, moaned the dove. "I have to scratch and search to find any food at all."

"Too bad," said Akoko. "Look at me. See how fat I am! I have become a person of some importance."

"What does it mean to be a person of some importance?" asked Aturukuku.

Kut-kut-kut, clucked the hen. "Come at dusk, and you will see how my mistress fusses over me and brings me food—as if I were a queen!"

"But why are you tied to the tree?" asked the dove.

"To keep me here, I suppose," said the hen.

Aturukuku flew off. At dusk she returned. The rope under the tree was empty. And a cat lay near the place where the hen had been.

"Where is Akoko?" cried the dove.

"Oh," said the cat, "she was fat enough. So our mistress put her into the cooking pot."

A-kuu, a-kuu mourned the dove. And she flew off saying, "It is better to be free—even if you have to scratch for a living and never become a person of some importance."

AFTERWORD

This is a fable about freedom, and it has special significance because it was recorded during the period when the Gold Coast was a British colony and the Ashanti were not free in their own land. Chickens had long been domesticated in West Africa, so to the Ashanti, the hen was a metaphor for themselves under British rule.

This fable was discovered by Captain Robert S. Rattray, a British government official who helped the people of the Gold Coast win limited political freedoms in the early 1900s. Rattray was the head of the Department of Anthropology for the colonial government and believed that knowledge of national folklore and customs was essential for a good, responsible government.

On March 26, 1957, the Gold Coast was reborn as Ghana. Since then, like Aturukuku the dove, the Ashanti have been free.

GLOSSARY

Fang: A Bantu-speaking tribe from west-central Africa

Sloogey dog: Probably a saluki

Hungry country: The desert

Vex: A tantrum

Kiboko (kee-BOH-koh): A rhinoceros hide whip

Ee, ee (AY, AY): Yes, yes

THE SLOOGEY DOG
AND THE STOLEN AROMA

A FANG TALE

THERE WAS ONCE A GREEDY AFRICAN WHO THROUGH SHREWD AND SOME-times dishonest dealings had become very rich. He was so rich in ivory that he had a fence of tusks all around his compound. He was so rich in sheep that he dared not count them, lest the evil spirits become jealous and destroy them.

He had so many wives that it took him from sunup to sundown just to walk past the doors of their huts. And he had so many daughters of marriageable age that he kept them in a band, guarded day and night by old women.

The favorite pastime of this rich man was eating. But no guest ever dipped a finger in the pot with him, and no pet sat near him waiting for fallen crumbs.

He ate alone in the shade of a big tree near the ivory gate of his compound. He ate much food and he became very fat.

One day as he sat on his eating stool, a procession of wives filed over to him from the cookhouse. Each carried on her head a basket or platter or bowl of food. Each put her offering before him and backed away to sit on her heels and watch him eat. Among the delicacies this day were baked elephant's foot, fried locusts, and rice balls with peanut gravy. A wonderful aroma rose from the steaming food. It flooded the compound and seeped through the ivory fence.

Now it happened that at the very moment the smell was spreading through the jungle, the Sloogey Dog was coming down a nearby path. In her wanderings, she had foolishly crossed the hot, barren "hungry country" and she was truly on the verge of starvation.

When the smell of the rich man's food met her, her head jerked up and saliva gathered at the corners of her mouth. New strength came into her long, lean body. She trotted, following the scent, straight to the rich man's gate.

The Sloogey Dog pushed on the gate. It was tied fast. So she peered between the ivory posts. Seeing the man eating meat off a bone, she made polite little begging sounds deep in her throat, *mmm, mmm, mmm.* Saliva dribbled from her mouth in two long threads.

The sight of the hungry creature at his very gate spoiled the rich man's appetite. He threw a vex and bellowed, "Get away from my face, beggar!"

The Sloogey Dog was outside the fence, where anyone had a right to be. She knew she did not have to go away. But she had another

idea. She trotted all the way around the compound searching for the pile of rich scraps which she thought would be somewhere near the fence. She found not so much as a peanut shuck.

However, she did not forget the wonderful aroma of that food. Each day at mealtime she came to sniff and beg and drool at the rich man's gate. Each day the man drove her away. And each day his anger grew—until finally he left his food and went straight to the Council of Old Men.

He told his story. Then he said, "I want you to arrest that beggar of a dog!"

"On what grounds?" asked the oldest man.

"For stealing the aroma of my food!" said the rich man.

So, although she had broken no law, the dog was arrested, a judge was appointed, and a day was set for the trial.

On the day of the trial, the whole village gathered about the Tree of Justice. From the start, the sympathy of the people was with the Sloogey Dog—there was scarcely one of them who had not been swindled by the rich man.

But the judge was a just man. "I agree that the aroma was part of the food and so belonged

to the accuser," he said. "And since the dog came every day, she did it intentionally."

Murmurs of pity came from the crowd.

The Sloogey Dog yawned nervously, *ah-roooo-ow!*

The judge continued, "If she had stolen only once, the usual punishment would be to cut off her paws."

The Sloogey Dog's legs gave way under her, and she slithered on her belly to a hiding place behind the Tree of Justice.

"However," said the judge, "since the crime was a daily habit, I must think about it overnight before I decide on a suitable punishment."

The Sloogey Dog spent a miserable night.

Bad dreams plagued her—dreams so horrid that her legs jerked, her body shuddered, and she whined in her sleep. By morning she was exhausted.

At sunup the people gathered to hear the sentence. In came the judge, leading a horse. He dropped the reins to the ground and left the animal standing near the open gate to the village.

Was the horse part of the punishment? Was the judge taking a trip later? He only shrugged when people questioned him.

The judge called the rich man and the Sloogey Dog to come before him. Handing a kiboko to the rich man, he said, "The accused will be beaten to death by the accuser!"

The dog flinched as if the whip had already come down upon her back!

The rich man took off his gold-embroidered robe. He whipped the kiboko through the air in a practice swing.

The judge held up his hand. "Wait!" he commanded. Then, turning to the people, he asked, "Do the people agree that it was the invisible part of the food, and therefore its spirit, that was stolen?"

"Ee, ee!" cried the villagers.

The judge raised his hand again. "Do you, the people, agree that the spirit of the dog is her shadow?"

"Ee, ee!" they cried.

"Then," boomed the judge, "since the crime was against the spirit of the food, only the spirit of the dog shall be punished!"

The people howled with laughter. They slapped each other's backs and drummed their feet on the hard-packed earth.

The Sloogey Dog leaped up and licked the judge's nose.

The judge turned to the rich man, and when he could be heard, he said, "The shadow is big now. But you must beat it until the sun is straight up in the sky. When there is nothing left of the shadow, we shall agree that it is dead."

The rich man threw down the whip, picked up his garment, and said, "I withdraw the charges."

The judge shook his head. "You caused the arrest," he said. "You wanted the trial. Now administer justice! And if the kiboko touches so much as a hair of the Sloogey Dog, it will be turned upon you!"

There was nothing for the rich man to do but swing the whip hour after hour. The people watched and laughed as the dog leaped and howled, pretending to suffer with her shadow.

As the sun rose higher and higher, the shadow became smaller and smaller—and much harder to hit. The whip became heavier in the man's flabby hands. He was dripping with sweat and covered with dust stirred up by the whip. When he could hardly bear the ordeal any longer, the dog lay down. Then, to keep from touching a hair, the man had to get on his knees

and put one arm between himself and the dog. When he brought the whip down, it struck his arm.

Murmurs of satisfaction came from the crowd—"Good! Good! That's what he deserves!"

The rich man bellowed and threw the kiboko. Then he ran to the judge's horse, climbed onto it, and rode headlong out of the village.

"He won't come back," said the oldest old man. "He would get his paws chopped off if he did. He stole the judge's horse!"

Then the Sloogey Dog slunk off toward the rich man's house, her long nose sniffing for a whiff of something cooking beyond the ivory gate.

AFTERWORD

This tale comes from Louise Stinetorf's *Beyond the Hungry Country,* a novel about a missionary family stationed among the Fang people in west-central Africa, a region that includes Cameroon, Equatorial Guinea, and Gabon. It was woven into the plot as a tale told by the family's cook and may actually be a Fang tribal tale.

One clue, however, points to a more ancient origin. The word *Sloogey* is believed to be a corruption of saluki, the name of a breed of hunting dog used by ancient Egyptians.

The descriptions of the rich man's wealth are exaggerations from the fertile imagination of the African storyteller. But it is true that in most polygamous African families each wife would have her own separate hut. And baked elephant's foot really was a wealthy man's delicacy!

GLOSSARY

Khoikhoi (KOI-koi): a people of southern Africa whose name means "men of men." Formerly nomadic herders, most Khoikhoi now live in urban areas or on official reserves in South Africa and Namibia.

THE COCK AND THE JACKAL

A KHOIKHOI FABLE

ONE DAY A COCK WAS CAUGHT BY A JACKAL. THE JACKAL WAS ABOUT TO kill him, when the cock said, "Go ahead. Kill me, Jackal. But please *pray* before you eat me—as man does."

Jackal asked, "What does it mean to *pray?*"

Cock said, "Man folds his hands—like this. And he says, 'Thank you, God, for what I am about to eat.'"

Jackal thought if man did it, it must be a wise thing to do. He put his forepaws together, as the cock had indicated, and he said, "Thank you,

47

God, for this chicken I am about to eat."

"That was good," said Cock. "But you were looking around. Man closes his eyes when he prays. Try again."

The jackal prayed again—this time with his eyes closed. And the cock flew up into a nearby tree. From a safe perch, he called, "You foolish jackal! Next time, keep your eyes open, and don't try to be what you are not!"

48

AFTERWORD

This fable was discovered in the middle of the seventeenth century by the missionary Dr. Wilhelm Bleek. It shows a Christian influence, and Dr. Bleek said that it may have originated in Europe, with the jackal replacing Reynard the Fox, since there are no foxes in southern Africa. Tales about foxes first appeared in Europe in the eleventh century, and *The Epic of Reynard the Fox* is a collection of those tales. In one of them, the fox grabs a cock and is pursued by the protesting farmer. The cock says to the fox, "Tell him I am yours, not his." When the fox opens his mouth to speak, the cock escapes.

In the old days, the Khoikhoi (KOI-koi), from whom this tale was obtained, roamed the plains of southwestern Africa with their cattle and chickens. They had only temporary homes, so the women did not plant gardens, but rather helped with the animals. The Khoikhoi drank sweet milk, unlike the Zulu, who made *amasi* (cottage cheese) of theirs, and the Masai, who mixed theirs with fresh blood drawn from the necks of their cows.

GLOSSARY

Boconono (BOH-coh-NOH-noh): The word means *of the weasel family.*

Zulu (ZOO-loo): The word means *heaven*. The Zulus live in southeastern Africa, between the western escarpment of the Drakensburg Mountains and the Indian Ocean.

Tlick: A sound made by clicking the tongue

Hau (HAH-oo): An expression of aversion

Ugwali (ug-WAH-lee): A simple musical instrument made by attaching a short hollow quill to one end of a bowstring. Humming into the quill vibrates the string, producing a kazoolike sound.

Umdiandiane (um-de-AHN-de-AHN-ay): An edible root that grows wild in South Africa

Puo (POO-oh): An exclamation of surprise

Impis (IM-pees): Warriors

NO, BOCONONO!

A ZULU TALE

LONG AGO, IN ZULULAND, THE WIFE OF A KING GAVE BIRTH TO A STRANGE child. When the midwife saw him, she clicked her tongue, *tlick, tlick,* and said, "This is not a baby. It is a little man!"

The queen looked at the little fellow with a head too large for his body, and the face of an adult. She said, "Hau! He is odd. But he is still my child."

Although just born, the infant could walk and talk. He scampered about the hut, touching things and peeping into pots and baskets, saying, "What's this? What's this?"

"Yo!" cried the queen. "He's like a curious little weasel. I shall call him Boconono."

When the king saw Boconono, he cried, "This is no child! This is a dwarf! We must get rid of him. He will bring us nothing but trouble!"

51

The queen said, "What trouble could be worse than having no child at all?"

So they kept Boconono. But life was difficult for the little fellow. He wanted to be accepted by the people of the village. But everyone, except the queen, teased him.

When he begged to go hunting with the men, they would say, "No, Boconono. You are too small. A lion might eat you—a baby lion!" And they would laugh.

When he wanted to go out with the boys to herd cattle, they would say, "No, Boconono. You are too little. The cows would step on you!" And they would laugh.

Boconono made himself a small ugwali. And he played such marvelous tunes on it that eventually the herdboys let him come along. Out on the hills, he would entertain them, and it seemed that even the cows were soothed by his melodies.

One day there was a wedding in a neighbor-

ing town. All the impis of the village went to it in their plumed headdresses and their best finery. The king and queen went too, and the young women and even the old men.

But when Boconono asked to go, they said, "No, Boconono. You are too small. Besides, you don't have a spear of your own."

So Boconono was left behind with the grandmothers and the babies. More than anything in the world, he wanted to go and dance at that wedding. At last he decided to go all by himself. First he put on a headdress and his best leopard-fur kilt. Then, taking up his ugwali, he set out for the village where the wedding was being held.

When Boconono arrived, the drums were beating:

Kra, ka, ka, hi!
Gada, gada, gada.
Kra, ka, ka, hi!
Gada, gada, gada.

Men were dancing in a circle, hopping on one foot and then the other—tossing their plumed heads and brandishing their spears.

Boconono slipped into the circle. He hopped on one foot and then the other, bobbing his head and waving his ugwali.

The man behind him yelled, "Boconono, you can't dance with an ugwali. Get a spear!"

So Boconono left, saying to himself, "How can I get a spear? I must get one! Then I can dance at the wedding." He set out at once. Soon he spotted an umdiandiane plant on a little knoll. He dug up the root of it and said, "Now I have something. But an umdiandiane won't buy a spear."

Farther on, Boconono came to a house. He asked the woman there to cook his root for him. She said, "I will cook it, Little Man. But you must share it with me."

Boconono sat in the shade of the hut and played his ugwali while he waited for the root to cook. When it was done, the woman tasted it. It was so sweet, she ate it all.

Now the aroma of the cooked umdiandiane came to Boconono. He called, "Bring me my root."

"I can't," said the woman. "I ate my half and, PUO, your half followed it right down my throat!"

Boconono said:

"Pay me, pay me, pay me
For my umdiandiane;
The root I dug up on a little knoll,
When they wouldn't let me dance
At the wedding."

So the woman gave him a wooden milk pail in payment. "Thank you," said the little man. Then he went on his way, tootling his ugwali: *OO, oo; OO-oo-OO; oo, oo . . .*

Soon he came upon a boy who was milking a goat into a broken bowl. He said, "Here, take this pail of mine. Milk into it, and give a drink of milk to me."

The herdboy milked into the wooden pail. But as he carried it to Boconono to let him drink, it slipped out of his fingers. And KWOK! It broke on the hard ground.

Boconono said:

"Pay me, pay me, pay me
For my milk pail;
The pail the woman gave me;
The woman who ate my umdiandiane;
The root I dug up on a little knoll,
When they wouldn't let me dance
At the wedding."

The herdboy gave Boconono a stone knife. "Thank you," said the little man. And he went on his way, tootling his ugwali: *OO, oo; OO-oo-OO; oo, oo* . . .

Boconono had not gone far, when he saw a man slicing liver with a sliver of dry sugar cane. He said, "Grandfather, use this knife of mine. And when you have finished using it, give a slice of meat to me."

The old man used Boconono's knife. But as he was cutting a thick part, *kirik,* the knife broke!

Boconono said:

"Pay me, pay me, pay me
For my stone knife;
The knife the herdboy gave me;
The herdboy who broke my milk pail;
The pail the woman gave me;
The woman who ate my umdiandiane;
The root I dug up on a little knoll,
When they wouldn't let me dance
At the wedding."

The old man gave Boconono an ax.

"Thank you," said the little man. And he went on his way, tootling his ugwali: *OO, oo; OO-oo-OO; oo, oo* . . .

Soon he came upon an old woman breaking up firewood with her feet. He asked, "Grandmother, have you no ax? Here, take this one of mine. And when you have finished, give it back to me."

The old woman took the ax. But as she was chopping, the head of it loosened and flew off into a thicket. And it could not be found.

Boconono said:

"Pay me, pay me, pay me
For my ax;
The ax the old man gave me;
The old man who broke my knife;
The knife the herdboy gave me;
The herdboy who broke my milk pail;
The pail the woman gave me;
The woman who ate my umdiandiane;
The root I dug up on a little knoll,
When they wouldn't let me dance
At the wedding."

The woman gave Boconono an old cowhide blanket.

"Thank you," said the little man. Then he went on his way, tootling his ugwali: *OO, oo; OO-oo-OO; oo, oo* . . .

Farther on, Boconono came upon two impis who were lying under a tree without any covering. He asked, "Friends, have you no blanket?

Here, take this one of mine. And I shall come for it in a little while."

The young men covered themselves with the blanket. But it was very old and brittle, and much too small. They kept pulling it from one to the other. And they tore it in many places.

When Boconono came for it, he saw what they had done. He said:

"Pay me, pay me, pay me
For my blanket;
The blanket the old woman gave me;
The old woman who broke my ax;
The ax the old man gave me;
The old man who broke my knife;
The knife the herdboy gave me;
The herdboy who broke my milk pail;
The pail the woman gave me;
The woman who ate my umdiandiane;
The root I dug up on a little knoll,
When they wouldn't let me dance
At the wedding."

The impis gave Boconono a dagger. It was just the right size for a spear.

"Thank you! Thank you!" cried the little man. And he went dancing his way back to the village, where the wedding was still in full swing.

When he arrived, the drums were beating:

Kra, ka, ka, hi!
Gada, gada, gada.
Kra, ka, ka, hi!
Gada, gada, gada.

The impis were still dancing in a circle, hopping on one foot, then the other—tossing their plumed heads and brandishing their spears.

Boconono slipped into the circle. He hopped on one foot, then the other. He tossed his plumed head and brandished his little spear.

The queen saw him, and she cried, "Yo, yo, yo! Look at Boconono!"

The little man heard her. He waved his spear at her, and answered, "Yo, yo, yo!"

And nobody said, "No, Boconono." Because now he was a little impi, with a small spear of his own.

NO, BOCONONO!

AFTERWORD

Boconono—also called Hlakanyana (HAH-lah-kahn-YAH-nah)—is a legendary dwarf sometimes called the Tom Thumb of the Zulu. This is one of the many Boconono tales that Dr. Henry Calloway included in a reading textbook he wrote. Before then, the Bible was the only book published in Zulu, a language in the Bantu family.

Whether they came from a common source or sprang up independently, dwarf stories appear in the folklore of many lands. The European "Tom Thumb" was included in Charles Perrault's book *Tales of Mother Goose*, published in 1697—171 years before the publication of the Zulu dwarf tales. And the most famous dwarfs of all, the seven in the Grimm brothers' "Snow White," also preceded the Zulu stories.

Meanwhile, in the lore of the North American Indians and the Eskimo, little people had already found a place. The pukwudjinnies (puk-wud-JIN-nies) were old men no larger than papooses. In an Ojibwa legend, they save a beautiful young maiden from having to marry an old war chief by turning her into a pine tree.

GLOSSARY

Kanuri (Kahn-YOO-ree): A tribe whose men tend
the cattle and whose women farm the land

TOAD'S TRICK

A KANURI FABLE

A FABLE! A FABLE! BRING IT! BRING IT!

One morning a toad said to a rat, "I can do something that you can't do."

"What?" cried the rat. "You don't even know how to run. You just throw yourself, *lop*—and then you stop and look around."

Toad said, "You see those men sitting under that ficus tree? I will go right through the middle of them without being harmed. If *you* can do that, I will eat my words."

Then *lop, lop, lop* went the toad toward the men under the tree.

"Ah, there's a toad," said one of the men.

"Do not harm it," said another. "Toads eat bugs."

And the toad hopped in a leisurely manner between the stools of the men, and returned to the rat by a different way.

Then the rat set out with great speed, *kipido, kipido, kipido*—straight for the group of men.

"A rat!" yelled one of the men. "Get him!"

In and out among the stools scrambled the rat. The men tried to step on him. They tried to stomp him with the legs of their stools. Finally a man struck him with a stick and chased him into the forest, whacking him again and again!

Later, when the rat returned to the toad, he said, "You were right. There is something you can do that I cannot."

And that is true for all of us—there are some things that only we can do.

That is it. Put it on top of the granary.

AFTERWORD

This Kanuri fable is retold from the second book of African folklore ever published in English: an 1854 textbook written by Rev. S. W. Koelle. The text was used in mission schools in what is now Zambia.

As in this tale, it is typical in Kanuri culture that during the daytime the men would sit under trees while the women worked in their huts or gardens. A "wise saying" from the time of Koelle's book reveals the tribe's attitude toward women: "Who are more in number, men or women?" The answer: "Women, because men who listen to what women say are counted as women."

Kanuri storytellers often began by announcing, "A story! A story!" or "A fable! A fable!" The audience would respond with the cry "Bring it! Bring it!" And at the end of the tale, the narrator would say, "Put it on top of the granary"—which means "Add this to your store of stories."

GLOSSARY

Swahili (Swah-HE-le): The word means *coast people*, and designates descendants of Arabs who intermarried with native Africans

Zanzibar (ZAHN-zi-BAR): A large tropical island off the coast of Tanzania (Tahn-za-NE-ah), East Africa, a country formed by the union of Tanganyika and Zanzibar

Calabash (CAL-a-bash): A gourd that grows on a tropical tree, the dried shell of which is used for fashioning cups, bottles, and bowls

GOSO the TEACHER

A SWAHILI NARRATIVE POEM

THE TALE OF GOSO THE TEACHER
HAS COME FROM AFAR,
FROM THE AFRICAN ISLAND
OF ZANZIBAR

GOSO THE TEACHER

One day Goso's classroom
    was unbearably hot,
So he went out to look for
    a comfortable spot.

The place that he found
    was shady and cool,
But it turned out to be
    very bad for a school.

This is the tree with
    the big calabashes
Where Goso decided
    to teach his classes.

These are the children,
    his pupils, who really
Were reading and writing
    in native Swahili;
Under the tree with
    the big calabashes,
Where Goso decided
    to teach his classes.

64

This is the gourd that
    fell on his head,
Leaving him lying
    as if he were dead—

Right there in front of
    his pupils, who really
Were reading and writing
    in native Swahili;
Under the tree with
    the big calabashes,
Where Goso decided
    to teach his classes.

This is the monkey,
    up in the tree,
Who hurried off saying,
    "They'll prob'ly blame me
For dropping the calabash
    on the man's head!"
Leaving him lying
    as if he were dead—

Right there in front of
    his pupils, who really
Were reading and writing
    in native Swahili;

Under the tree with
    the big calabashes,
Where Goso decided
    to teach his classes.

This is the breeze
    that broke the stem
And sent the calabash
    crashing on him!
So the innocent monkey,
    up in the tree,
Hurried off saying,

"They'll prob'ly blame me
For dropping the calabash
    on the man's head!"
Leaving him lying
    as if he were dead—

Right there in front of
    his pupils, who really
Were reading and writing
    in native Swahili;

Under the tree with
    the big calabashes,
Where Goso decided
    to teach his classes.

This is the wall that
    steered the breeze
Over and up to the
    tops of the trees;
The breeze that broke
    the brittle stem
And sent the calabash
    crashing on him!
So the innocent monkey,
    up in the tree,
Hurried off saying,
    "They'll prob'ly blame me
For dropping the calabash
    on the man's head!"
Leaving him lying
    as if he were dead—

Right there in front of
    his pupils, who really
Were reading and writing
    in native Swahili;
Under the tree with
    the big calabashes,
Where Goso decided
    to teach his classes.

This is the merchant
    who built the wall—
To protect his property,
    that was all;

The wall that chanced
    to steer the breeze
Over and up to the
    tops of the trees;
The breeze that broke
    the brittle stem
And sent the calabash
    crashing on him!

So the innocent monkey,
    up in the tree,
Hurried off saying,
    "They'll prob'ly blame me
For dropping the calabash
    on the man's head!"
Leaving him lying
    as if he were dead—

Right there in front of
    his pupils, who really
Were reading and writing
    in native Swahili;
Under the tree with
    the big calabashes,
Where Goso decided
    to teach his classes.

GOSO THE TEACHER

When the merchant and others
    had gathered around,
Goso opened his eyes and
    sat up on the ground.
With his hand he explored
    the lump on his head,
And he said to the people,
    "I'm glad I'm not dead!"
Now Goso the teacher
    is teaching his classes
In the shade of a tree
    that has *no* calabashes.

AFTERWORD

Originally told in Swahili, this cumulative tale was first translated into English in the 1890s by George W. Bateman, the administrator of a boys' school in Zanzibar.

The original source story was not told in rhyme. Instead, it takes the form of a question-and-answer session, allowing for lively interaction between the storyteller and his audience. The teller begins by blaming the wind for knocking loose the calabash. The audience responds by pretending to punish the wind with a beating.

"Why do you beat me?" the wind asks. "What have I done?" The audience replies, "You threw down the calabash that struck our teacher Goso."

The wind then blames the wall, and the listeners "beat" the wall, and so on, until nine more episodes are finished.

GLOSSARY

Hapendeki (Hah-pen-DAY-kee): Swahili name

Binti (BIN-tee): Swahili name

Bibi (BEE-bee): Swahili for *lady*

Baba (BAH-bah): Swahili for *father*

Muscat (Mus-CAHT): A seaport city on the mainland

La: Swahili for *no*

Kanga (KAHN-ga): A dress

Jambo (ZHAHM-boh): Swahili for *hello*

Papo hapo (PAH-poh HAH-poh): Swahili for *immediately*

Viv-yo hiv-yo (VEEV-yoh HEEV-yoh): Swahili for *the same way*

Kanzu (KAHN-zoo): The long white linen garment worn by
    Moslem men

Allah (AH-lah): The Supreme Being of the Moslems

HAPENDEKI AND BINTI THE BIBI

A SWAHILI TALE

LONG AGO ON THE ISLAND OF ZANZIBAR, A CERTAIN MAN AND HIS wife has seven sons. And they named the seventh one Hapendeki.

One day the seventh son said to his father, "Baba, what goal in life is there for a man?"

His father replied, "One goal is to find a good woman and marry her."

Hapendeki said, "Then, Baba, you must find a wife for me."

"You are too young," said his father. "You would never be able to manage a wife."

"Hmmm," said Hapendeki to himself. "Sometimes you have to peel your own bananas." To his father he said, "All right. If you won't find a wife for me, I'll find one for myself."

Hapendeki set out at once. He searched every town on the island. At last he found a girl who was so beautiful and so poised that people called her Binti the Bibi. He lost no time in asking her to marry him. He promised, "If you will be my wife, I'll give you everything your heart desires."

The two were married, and they had a grand wedding. Then, after they had stayed indoors the required time for a honeymoon, Binti the Bibi said, "Now, my husband, I want some very nice clothes to wear to show myself off when I go about once more."

Hapendeki went to the shops of the Indian merchants and he gathered one man's load of lovely garments.

72

But when Binti opened the bundle, she said, "Do you call these beautiful? They are too ordinary. I can't show myself off in these."

So Hapendeki took a ship to Muscat, and there he bought the most expensive kangas and turbans in the city—all made of silk and embroidered in many colors.

But when his wife saw them, she said, "La! Hapendeki, these are not what I want. And you promised to give me whatever I desired!"

Hapendeki said, "Binti, my wife, how can I please you? These are the finest clothes in all the markets of Muscat! Now tell me, what sort of garments do you want?"

Binti said, "I want something that nobody else has. I want a kanga made from the skin of Pemba Muhori."

Pemba Muhori was a great sea serpent. His skin was as smooth as silk and patterned in brilliant colors. But no man dared to attack him, because he had seven heads.

Hapendeki wanted to keep his promise. So he conceived a plan. First he went to the home of his parents and told them how his wife refused to wear any kanga that was not made from the skin of Pemba Muhori.

His father said, "Didn't I tell you that you would not be able to manage a wife?"

His brothers said, "You had to marry before we did—we, your older brothers! And this is what comes of it!"

"I don't want advice," said Hapendeki. "All I want is for Mama to bake me seven loaves of bread."

Hapendeki's mother baked the bread.

Then the next day he set out with his sword and the seven loaves. He traveled through swamps and forests, and at last he came to a very wide lake. There he stood at the edge of the water and sang:

"Jambo, Pemba Muhori!
Are you there?
My wife is wanting
your skin to wear."

Then, PAPO HAPO! There came a noise like thunder. Great waves foamed up to the shore. And out of one of them came the seven heads of Pemba Muhori—all of them writhing, *viv-yo, hiv-yo!* From all of his mouths at once, he roared, "Who is calling my name?"

The young man said, "It is I, Hapendeki. I have brought you some fresh-baked bread." He held out a crusty brown loaf to the first head. The ugly mouth opened, and he threw it right in. Then with one swift slash of his sword, he cut off that head.

The serpent came at him with his second head. Again Hapendeki threw in a loaf of bread

and chopped off that head. He did the same to the third, fourth, fifth, and sixth heads.

Then the serpent came at him with his last head, lashing his tail so furiously that the waves washed over Hapendeki's own head. But he managed to pop the last loaf into that horrible mouth and to cut off that head, too.

Next the young man dragged the heavy body up onto the grass and carefully removed the skin. After wrapping it in his kanzu, he set out for home. When he arrived, Binti saw that he had been successful, and she cried, "My brave husband, how did you manage to fight Pemba Muhori?"

"By the grace of Allah," said Hapendeki.

Binti the Bibi unwrapped the bundle. She spread out the skin, which glistened with bright colors in intricate designs. "It's beautiful!" she gasped. "Now let's hire a tailor and have him make me a kanga and a turban. And I shall have something that no other woman in the world has!"

Soon Binti the Bibi was parading everywhere in her exotic garments.

One day Hapendeki's mother said to him, "Was it worth it, my son, that you should risk your life so that your wife could flaunt herself like that?"

Hapendeki thought about that, and he said to himself, "I must teach Binti a lesson, or she may continue to put me to a lot of trouble." So the next day, when his wife brought him a drink of water, he said, "Binti, this water is not fit for me to drink!"

"What's wrong with it?" cried Binti.

"It smells of frogs," he said. "I want water from a lake in which no frogs live."

Binti protested, but at last she set out to find such a lake. The first body of water she came to looked clean and blue. She said, "Perhaps this water will do." But just as she was about to fill

her jar, a frog jumped into the water with a *lop*.

So Binti went on. All day she walked from lake to pond and pond to lake. But always she saw frogs sitting on water-soaked logs, or she heard them calling, *w-r-r-r, w-r-r-r, w-r-r-r*.

Finally she gave up and returned home. She put down the empty water jar in front of Hapendeki and said, "There's no body of water on the whole island that doesn't have frogs in it! See the trouble you have caused me!"

But Hapendeki said, "Look here, Binti, at least you didn't have to fight a serpent with seven heads!"

Binti began to cry. And Hapendeki gathered her into his arms and dried her tears. Then together they vowed that never again would they put any unnecessary hardship upon each other.

When Hapendeki's parents and his brothers heard about that, they decided that the youngest son had managed quite well after all.

And his mother said, "When one palm washes the other, the hands are clean."

AFTERWORD

The Swahili live on the island of Zanzibar and along most of the east coast of Africa, from Somalia to Mozambique. They are a Moslem people of mixed Arab and Bantu bloodlines. Swahili men were traders and they did the buying for their families, so it is not surprising that in this tale Hapendeki shopped for his wife's clothes. This story was set during a time of prosperity for the Swahili. Ships from China brought silk to seaports such as Muscat, an area renowned for its beautiful Swahili women, gorgeously dressed in silks and jewels. To get something for Binti that no one else had, Hapendeki was required to do something that no one else did.

GLOSSARY

Emo-Yo-Quaim (AY-moh-YOH-Quah-EEM): The black Jews
  of the Ondo jungle. The word means *strange people.*
Ondo (AHN-doh): A heavily forested state in western Nigeria
lalloped (LAH-lopt): An ideophone for *brachiated,* meaning
  swung by their arms from one handhold to the next

KINDAI AND THE APE
A TALE OF THE EMO-YO-QUAIM

IN A BAMBOO HUT INSIDE A BAM—
BOO FENCE IN THE ONDO BUSH, THERE
lived a man named Kindai. He lived with his
wife, Guhumaha, and their baby girl, Bekhor.

Kindai hunted in the jungle, and Guhumaha
raised peanuts, yams, and cassava in a garden
inside the fence. Food was plentiful. And
they felt quite safe in their compound—except
from apes who might be tempted to raid
their garden.

In another part of the jungle lived a troop of apes. There were a father, several wives, and many children of all ages, from babies to nearly full-grown juveniles. The big father ape was continually on guard, watching for snakes in the trees and men on the ground. The mothers, when they were not leading the family to patches of wild fruit, busied themselves with bending and weaving branches together to make beds in the trees. The troop was continually traveling, and new beds had to be made every day.

The children did nothing but play. They *lalloped*, from branch to branch and from tree to tree, *icking* and *ooing*. They played follow-the-leader and catch-me-if-you-can.

One day during a playful chase, a juvenile plummeted TAAA! out of a tree. He landed on a thorny branch. And a thorn broke off in his foot. He tried to scratch it out and to bite it out. But he could not remove the thorn.

For several days the injured ape stayed on

the ground, following his family who chattered above him in the trees. He ate fallen fruit and insects. By licking a stick and poking it into ant holes, he would catch stickfuls of the insects at one time.

One morning the ape's foot was so painful that he did not even try to follow his people. On one leg and the knuckles of his hands, he hobbled to a path. There he rested against a tree. Presently he saw a man approaching.

The man was Kindai. He saw the ape and raised his spear to hurl it. The animal grunted, *wuh, uh, uh,* and withdrew closer to the tree. Kindai was curious. He thought, Why doesn't he try to run away or to climb the tree?

Then Kindai saw the animal's swollen foot, with the black dot of a thorn in the middle of the swelling. He remembered how he had had a thorn in his foot one time, and how terribly it had hurt until Guhumaha removed it.

Kindai lowered his spear. Slowly he drew nearer to the animal, saying softly, "Little Brother of the Bush, I won't hurt you. If you will let me, I will help you."

The ape tipped his head sideways in a gesture of supplication, and he whimpered, *oo-oo-oo.* Then he let the man remove the thorn with a knife.

The pain must have been relieved at once, for the ape leaped away and shinnied partway up the tree. Then he stopped and looked back at Kindai as if to say thank you.

Kindai called to him. "Farewell, Little Brother of the Bush."

When Kindai told Guhumaha what he had done, she said, "Kindai, are you twins? How could one man be so foolish! The apes are our enemies! Now there will be one more left to raid our compound."

Bekhor cooed, *aaah*.

"See," said Guhumaha, "even the baby agrees with me."

After a time, the apes realized that their injured one was no longer following them, and they returned to look for him. How surprised they were to find him back high in a tree, and to hear that a man had helped him! His mother groomed him and said, "Some men are good."

Many moons later, in their travels, those apes came upon Kindai's bamboo hut and the garden inside the bamboo fence. The father dropped, *twum,* down onto the roof of the hut and began tearing up the thatch. The whole troop followed him into the compound, leaping from the trees that arched over the fence. They overran the garden, pulling up the plants.

Guhumaha grabbed a hoe, and brandishing it, she ran to the garden to frighten off the vandals.

A young ape saw her leave the hut, and he entered it. Inside, he went into a frenzy. He ripped a hammock from the wall, knocked

bowls and baskets off a shelf, and scattered the rolled-up mats.

Little Bekhor, who had been sleeping in her basket, woke up and began to scream. Attracted by her cries, and thinking of her as a trophy of war, the ape picked her up and made off with her.

Guhumaha heard the screams. She turned in time to see the big ape leap to an overhanging limb of a tree with the shrieking baby under one arm.

Now, Kindai had been hunting in the jungle nearby. He had heard the troop of apes as they went chattering through the treetops, traveling in the direction of his compound. He ran to try to head them off. As he entered the gate, he saw the huge father ripping up his roof. Kindai hurled his spear. It grazed the back of the big ape.

The animal howled with pain and leaped into the nearest tree. The others followed him, for apes will not fight without their leader. The raid was over.

But Guhumaha cried, "Kindai, one of them has run off with our baby!"

There followed a chase through the forest— the ape with the shrieking baby fleeing through the treetops, and Kindai and Guhumaha pursuing on the ground. The jungle was a tangle of bushes, vines, and fallen trees. Kindai, who was used to slashing his way through the undergrowth, was soon far ahead of his wife. And Guhumaha finally gave up and returned home.

But Kindai went on, struggling through or over or around obstacles in the way—following the sound of his baby's cries.

The ape could not travel well with his burden. And he was disturbed by the baby's screaming. At last he hunkered down in the crotch of a tree and rocked the child in his arms. He was gentle with her, for he had been taught by his mother never to harm an infant.

Kindai caught up with him there. He held out his arms and begged, "Little Brother of the Bush, please give back my baby!"

The ape cocked his head to one side, seeming to listen.

Kindai continued, "Little Brother of the Bush, I won't hurt you. Just give back my baby!"

Now, there was something familiar about the words or the voice that stirred memories in the mind of the animal. And he did a strange thing. He held out a scarred foot toward Kindai.

At once the man knew that this was the ape whom he had helped. He talked some more. And soon the animal was climbing down the long trunk of the tree with Bekhor tucked under one arm. When he was close enough, he gently dropped the baby into Kindai's outstretched arms. Then he muttered, *wuh-uh-uh-uh*, as he watched the man go off with his child nestled against his breast.

When Kindai arrived home, Guhumaha was overjoyed to see that he had saved the baby, and that she was unharmed.

But Kindai insisted, "I did not *save* Bekhor. The ape who stole her was the one who had the thorn in his foot. He *gave* Bekhor back to me!"

Then Guhumaha said, "It is a true saying—'If you do a good deed, the good will come back to you.'"

Little Bekhor snuggled in her mother's arms. And all that was left of her terror was the aftermath of tears, *ih-uh . . . ih-uh . . . ih-uh.*

AFTERWORD

This is a reciprocal tale with the universal theme of kindness rewarded, and it bears similarities to both Jewish and Roman legends. It originated with the Emo-Yo-Quaim, black Jews whose ancestors fled to northern Africa in A.D. 70, after the destruction of Jerusalem. After many generations, this tribe drifted to the south, settling in the Sahara Desert and mixing with the Berber people. Today, living in virtual isolation in the Ondo jungle, they still observe many Jewish traditions, and the moral of this tale reflects a Jewish ethic.

The story is also similar to the famous Roman legend about Androcles and the lion. According to that legend, when Androcles was thrown into a lion's den, the animal spared him because it recognized him as the man who had pulled a thorn from its paw many years before.

Apes are a special menace in the Ondo jungle. When they attack a village, they cannot be driven off until their leader is killed or injured.

BIBLIOGRAPHY

LEELEE GORO

"Leelee Goro" is a revision of "Goro, the Wonderful Wrestler" in *More Tales from the Story Hat,* by Verna Aardema, published by Coward–McCann, New York, 1966. The previous source is "Goro, the Wonderful Wrestler" in *Cunnie Rabbit, Mr. Spider, and the Other Beef,* by Florence M. Cronise and Henry W. Ward, published by Swan Sonnenchein, London, and by E. P. Dutton, New York, 1903; and reprinted by Afro-American Publishing Company, Chicago, 1969.

ANANSI AND THE PHANTOM FOOD

"Anansi and the Phantom Food" is retold from "The Discontented Spider" in a booklet entitled *Spider and Other Stories,* by Aunt Clara, published by Radio Station ELWA, Monrovia, Liberia, 1972.

THE BOOGEY MAN'S WIFE

"The Boogey Man's Wife" is retold from a story called "The Boogey Man and Da" in a booklet entitled *Mano Stories,* published by Literacy House, Monrovia, Liberia, 1952.

HALF-A-BALL-OF-KENKI

"Half-a-Ball-of-Kenki" is a revision of a story by the same name in *More Tales from the Story Hat,* Coward–McCann, 1966; and a picture book by the same name, published by Frederick Warne, 1979. The original source is "How Leopard's Body Became Spotted," in *Akan-Ashanti Folk-tales,* by R. S. Rattray, Oxford University Press, 1930; reprinted by AMS Press, New York, 1987.

THE HEN AND THE DOVE

"The Hen and the Dove" is retold from R. S. Rattray's book, *Akan–Ashanti Folk-tales,* Oxford University Press, 1930; reprinted by AMS Press, New York, 1987. This fable was published in *The Big Book Magazine,* Scholastic, Spring 1991.

THE SLOOGEY DOG AND THE STOLEN AROMA

"The Sloogey Dog and the Stolen Aroma" is a revision of a story by the same name in *Tales from the Story Hat,* by Verna Aardema, Coward–McCann, 1960. The previous source begins on page 214 in the novel *Beyond the Hungry Country,* by Louise Stinetorf, published by J. B. Lippincott, Philadelphia, PA, 1954. This tale was included in an anthology entitled *Time for Old Magic,* by May Hill Arbuthnot and Mark Taylor, published by Holt, Rinehart and Winston of Canada, 1986.

THE COCK AND THE JACKAL

"The Cock and the Jackal" is retold from "The Cock" in *Reynard the Fox in South Africa,* by Wilhelm H. I. Bleek, published by Trubner & Company, London, 1864; and reprinted by AMS Press, New York.

NO, BOCONONO!

"No, Boconono!" is retold from a story beginning on page 37 in *Nursery Tales, Traditions, and Histories of the Zulus, In Their Own Words, With a Translation into English, Volume 1,* by Henry Calloway, published by Trubner and Company, London, 1868; reprinted by Kraus Reprint and Periodicals, Millwood, N.Y., 1987.

TOAD'S TRICK

"Toad's Trick" is retold from Fable Number 8 in *African Native Literature,* by Sigismund W. Koelle, published by the Church Missionary House, London, 1854; and reprinted by Ayer Company Publishers, Salem, N.Y., no date.

GOSO THE TEACHER

"Goso the Teacher" is retold from a tale by the same title in George W. Bateman's book *Zanzibar Tales,* published by A. C. McClurg, Chicago, 1901; and reprinted by Afro-American Books, Chicago, 1969.

HAPENDEKI AND BINTI THE BIBI

"Hapendeki and Binti the Bibi" is retold from "Pemba Muhori" in *Black Tales for White Children,* by Chauncey and Mrs. Hugh Stigand, published by Houghton Mifflin, New York, 1914.

KINDAI AND THE APE

"Kindai and the Ape" is retold from a story by that name in *Tales for the Third Ear,* by Verna Aardema, published by E. P. Dutton, 1969. The original source is "The Man Who Thought He Was Foolish" in *Folktales of a Savage,* by Bata Kindai Amgoza Ibn Lobagola, published by Alfred A. Knopf, New York, 1930.